First Day
in
First Grade

MS. SHEILA EGBE

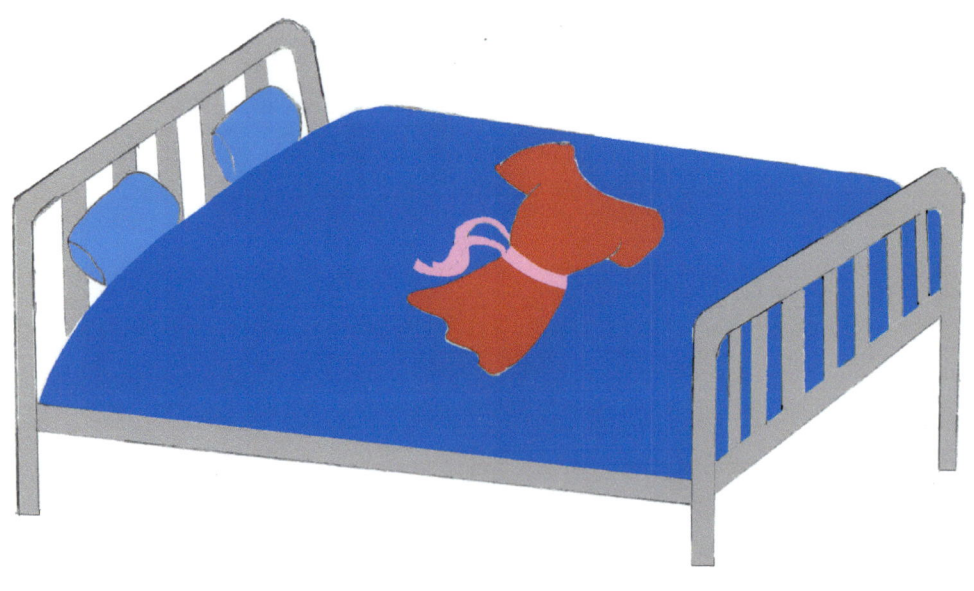

It was Brandi's first day of school in first grade, and she did not want to go to school. *Will the first graders like me,* she thought as she was getting ready for school.

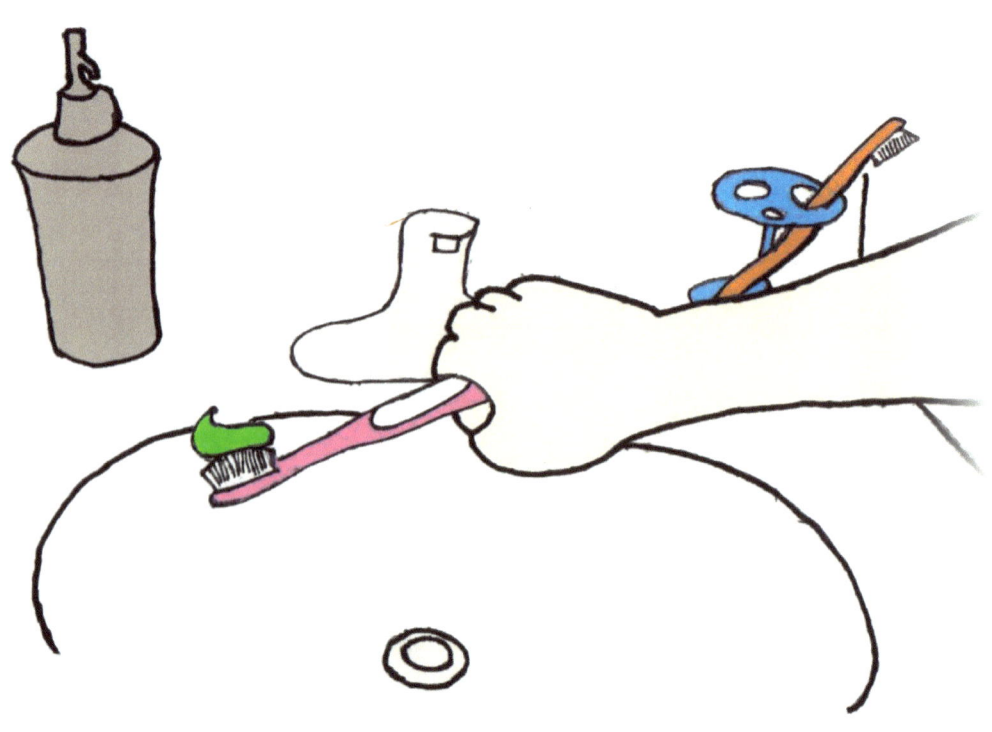

She took her pink toothbrush from the cup that the dentist had given to her. She put some green toothpaste on the brush and looked in the mirror. She gave herself a smile. *Maybe I should smile to the kids and they will like me.*

As she dressed, she heard Lizzy tell her to hurry up. Brandi wore her favorite red dress with the pink bow around the waist, and went downstairs for breakfast.

As Brandi ate her bowl of cereal, she swirled the cereal with her milk and watched the yellow school bus pick up little Sarah. Sarah would be going to first grade, too, but at another school. *Oh, how I wish I did not have to go to that new school, with all these new little boys and girls that I don't know,* she thought. *What am I going to say to them? Will I like them? Will they like me?*

"Come on; eat up," called Lizzy, "otherwise we will be late for school." Lizzy was starting the sixth grade in a new school, and she was not worried. It did not bother her that she was new to the school and had no friends there. "It's OK," Lizzy said. "I will make new friends."

Brandi grabbed her school bag and lunchbox with her peanut butter and jelly sandwich and walked toward the car. She sat in the car without saying a word to anyone. As the car got closer to her school, she looked through the window and saw all the boys and girls returning to school, too.

She saw little Dillon, who was in second grade. He held his sister's hand, who would also be going to first grade, just like Brandi. *Will she be in my class*, she thought.

Brandi got out of the car and waved goodbye to Lizzy. She walked up the stairs as she heard the principal blowing the whistle to prepare the kids for line-up.

Brandi stood in the hallway holding onto her pink lunchbox. She was a little scared to go inside, so she moved a little closer to the door and listened to the kids talk about their summer vacation.

Brandi pushed open the door and walked in. Everyone stopped talking and stared at her. "Good morning, boys and girls. My name is Brandi Egbe and I will be your first-grade teacher this year.

The boys and girls had huge smiles on their faces as they asked her lots of questions. Brandi realized that it was OK to be scared on her first day of school. She also knew that they would have lots of fun. She had a lot to learn from her first graders.